to Duncan, thank you for all your help

Text and cover design by Judith Robertson

Printed and bound in Singapore by Tien Wah Press
for the publishers Piccadilly Press Ltd,
5 Castle Road, London NW1 8PR

1 3 5 7 9 10 8 6 4 2

Typeset in Stone Serif

A catalogue record for this book is available from the British Library

ISBNs: 1 85340 504 3 paperback
1 85340 509 4 hardback

*Susan Hellard is an acclaimed illustrator who lives in North London.
Her illustrations have brought to life a myriad of characters, including
Dilly the Dinosaur. Sue won the Jean Piaget award with Anita Harper
for JUST A MINUTE for best integrated text and artwork. She is also the
author/illustrator of the first book in this series, BABY LEMUR.*

BABY LEMUR
ISBN: 1 85340 541 8 (p/b)
1 85340 546 9 (h/b)

BABY TIGER

Susan Hellard

Piccadilly Press • London

Deep in the darkest part of the forest,
Tozie the tiger, his sister Amber and
brother Toby were all born on the same day.
They were triplet tigers. Layla, their mother,
was very proud of them.

The triplets were all very small but Tozie was
the smallest. Layla fed them with her own milk,
and washed them with her rough tongue.

Sometimes she carried the cubs, one by one, with her huge teeth, but she never, ever hurt them.

The cubs grew bigger and bigger,
but Tozie remained the smallest.
Layla taught them all how to run
and pounce and catch things. She even taught
them how to swim. Tozie was so small, he found
it hard to keep up with his brother and sister.

But even though Tozie was the smallest cub,
he was the quickest at learning things: how to
hide in the thick jungle grasses, which sounds
and smells were good and which ones were bad,
which animals were friendly and which were not.

One night, when the moon was full,
Layla decided to take her cubs out
hunting with her for the first time.

This was the night that Tozie got into trouble!
The cubs followed their mother through the
forest. Tozie was not able to run as fast as
Amber and Toby and he got left behind.
Tozie was alone.

Just for a moment, he was frightened. Then he tried to think of the things his mother had taught him. Inside his head he could hear his mother's voice saying, "Stop and look, Tozie. What do you see?"

Tozie saw three paths twisting
away into the dark trees. He saw
claw marks on the tree-trunks,
so he knew his family had
been there. But which way
had they gone?

The night-time noises of the forest were all around Tozie. He knew his mother would say, "Stop and listen, Tozie. What do you hear?"

Tozie could hear the chattering of monkeys and the screech of peacocks. But the only sound he wanted to hear was his mother's growly voice!

Then Tozie remembered the most important thing his mother had taught him. "Stop and think, Tozie. And STAY RIGHT THERE!"
So Tozie looked for his mother with his eyes, and he listened with his ears, but he did not move from the spot.

Suddenly Tozie saw a flash of orange through the trees, and smelled a smell he loved. His mother!

With a leap and a bound, Layla was by his
side. Tozie gave a roar of delight so big that
it silenced the whole forest.

"You are a clever little cub, Tozie," Layla purred. "You stayed right where I could come back and find you." And his mother then nuzzled him with her nose, and Tozie stretched up as tall as he could on his hind legs and gave her the biggest lick he had ever given her in his life.

Tiger Facts

Tigers are the biggest members of the cat family.

They live mainly in the forests and grasslands of India.

They like to live alone.

The cubs live with their mother until they are about 18 months old.

Tiger mothers are very devoted mothers and very clean!

Cubs are almost blind for the first 2 months.

They suckle for the first few months.

The cubs leave the lair at about 6 months old, when they are fully weaned.

Tigers have wonderful eyesight and even better hearing.

The tigers' striped coats camouflage them well against tall grasses and shady forests.

They love to swim.